Whose Shoe?

by Margaret Miller

Greenwillow Books, New York

I want to thank all the children, grown-ups, and organizations who cheerfully put their best feet forward and made this book possible: Beth Basley, Adam Bass, Kerry Beck, Nicky Clifford, Kenya & Zelda Harris, Tarik Kitson, John Lindsay, Carlos & Noemi & Juan Carlos Lucero, Jessica Maginsky, New York Rangers, New York Yankees, Leonie Norton, Jenna Rappaport, Kate Reuther, Mika Sneddon, Sam Spector, William Watts, and Kate Zipser.

The full-color photographs were reproduced from 35-mm. Kodachrome 25 slides.

Library of Congress Cataloging-in-Publication Data
Miller, Margaret (date)
Whose shoe? / by Margaret Miller.
        p.   cm.
Summary: Illustrates a variety of footwear and matches
each wearer with the appropriate shoe.
ISBN 0-688-10008-2 (trade).   ISBN 0-688-10009-0 (lib.)
1. Shoes—Juvenile literature.   [1. Shoes.]
I. Title.   GT2130.M55   1991
391'.413—dc20   90-38491   CIP   AC

For my wonderful Kate

Whose shoe?

Baseball player

Whose shoe?

Clown

Whose shoe?

Baby

Whose shoe?

Ballet dancer

Whose shoe?

Horse

Whose shoe?

Hockey player

Whose shoe?

Swimmer

Whose shoe?

Runner

Whose shoe?

Angler

THE SHOES

Baseball cleat

Hockey skate

Clown shoe

Flipper

Baby shoe

Running shoe

Ballet slipper

Hip wader

Horseshoe